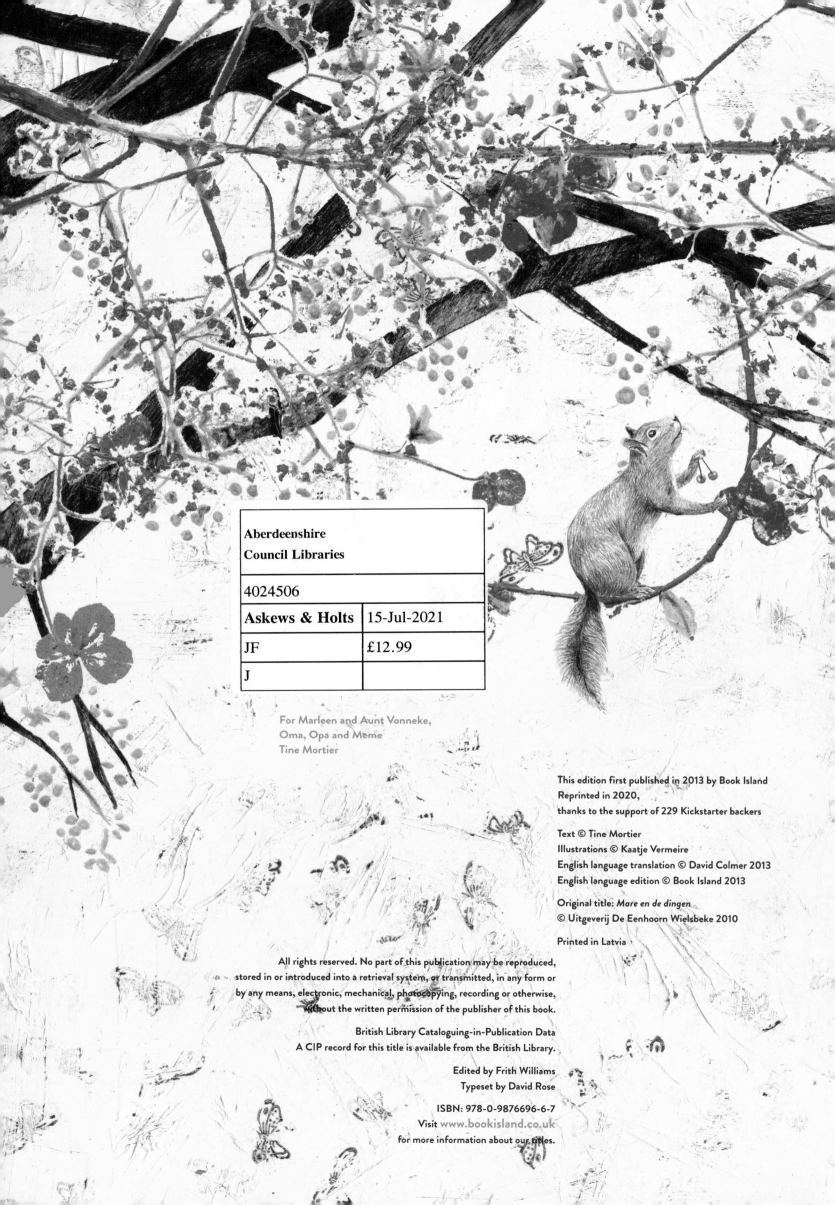

For Marleen and Aunt Vonneke,
Oma, Opa and Meme
Tine Mortier

This edition first published in 2013 by Book Island
Reprinted in 2020,
thanks to the support of 229 Kickstarter backers

Text © Tine Mortier
Illustrations © Kaatje Vermeire
English language translation © David Colmer 2013
English language edition © Book Island 2013

Original title: *Mare en de dingen*
© Uitgeverij De Eenhoorn Wielsbeke 2010

Printed in Latvia

British Library Cataloguing-in-Publication Data
A CIP record for this title is available from the British Library.

Edited by Frith Williams
Typeset by David Rose

ISBN: 978-0-9876696-6-7

Visit www.bookisland.co.uk
for more information about our titles.

Tine Mortier
Kaatje Vermeire

Translated by David Colmer

Maia
and What Matters

BOOK ISLAND

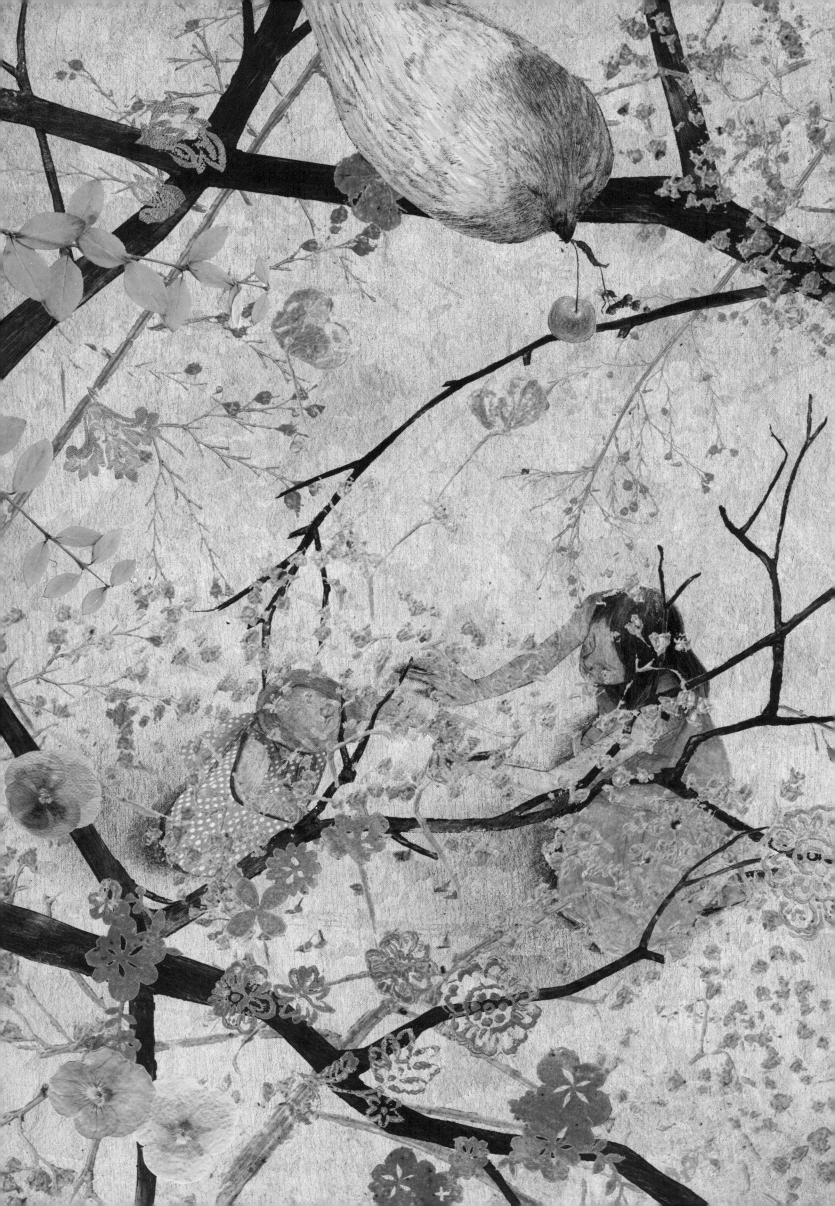

Maia was born under the cherry tree in a wicker chair.
Her mother was reading. It was an exciting book. So exciting
that at first she didn't realise the baby was coming. Like when
you're busting to go and think, 'I'll just hang on for a sec.'

Hang on for a sec? No way!

Maia didn't have an ounce of patience.

Let me out! Now!

She pressed and pushed and kicked until she was there.

Maia grew very quickly.

By six months, she was running around the garden. From the cherry
tree to the fence, once around the pond and back again.

Did you see how fast I was? Huh? Did you see? Nobody's that fast!

A few months later, she said her first word. Not 'mama' or 'dada'
but 'cake'. Maia was always hungry.

'Cake,' she said. **NOW!**

And she scoffed the lot.

Grandma was Maia's best friend. She was just as impatient as her
granddaughter and just as greedy.

When Grandma came to visit, it was one big party. They'd run around the
garden together. From the cherry tree to the fence, once around the pond
and back again. Then they'd eat a whole cake.

Have you ever had this much fun before?

Isn't this the yummiest cake ever?

Maia and Grandma climbed up into the cherry tree and yelled at the birds.

Stop pecking holes in our cherries!

They told each other stories and ate biscuits and sweets until they were
sticky with sugar and covered in crumbs.

One day, Grandma was lying on the ground. She'd stumbled,
said Grandpa. Maia didn't believe a word of it.

They're lying. Lying through their teeth.

Grandma never stumbled. Not over the gnarled roots of the oak,
not over the fence, and not over the loose stones halfway down
the path to the pond.

Grandma had fallen into a deep sleep. So deep she couldn't
wake up to run, eat, or tell stories.

Wake up, Grandma! Now!

But it didn't help.

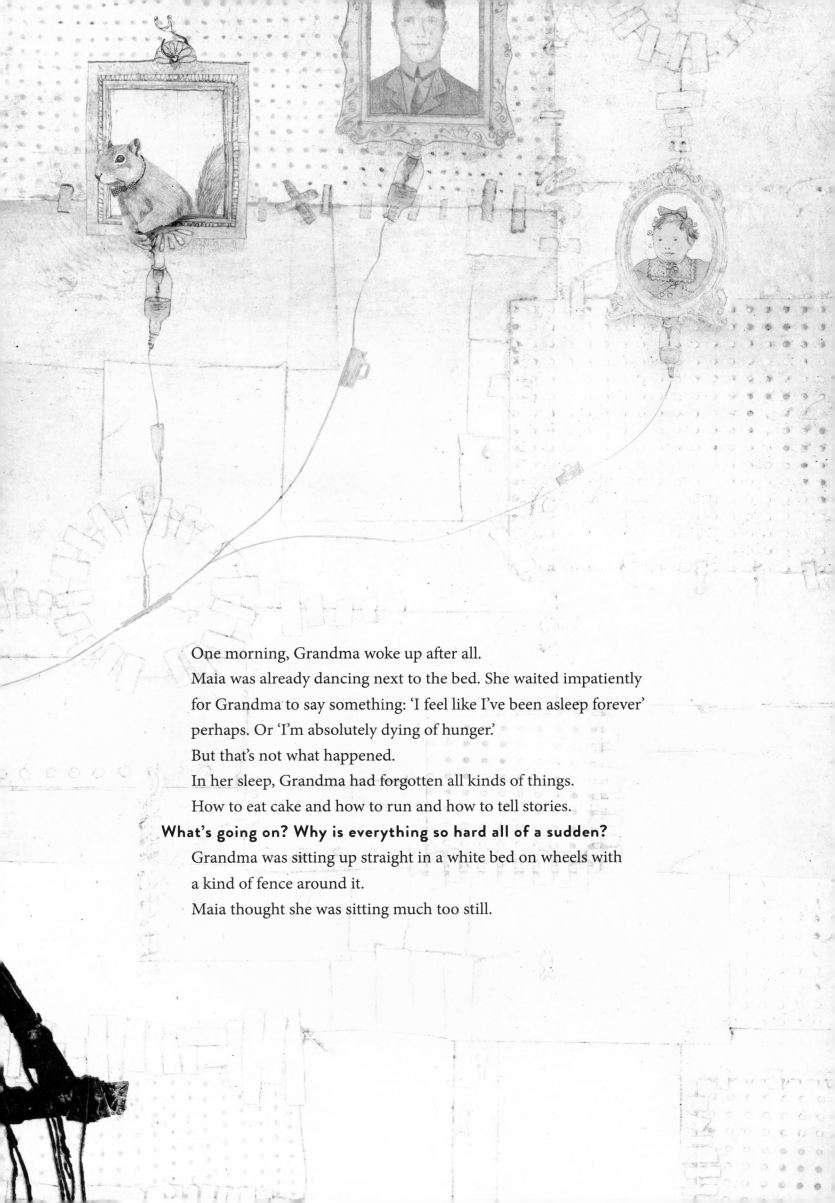

One morning, Grandma woke up after all.

Maia was already dancing next to the bed. She waited impatiently
for Grandma to say something: 'I feel like I've been asleep forever'
perhaps. Or 'I'm absolutely dying of hunger.'

But that's not what happened.

In her sleep, Grandma had forgotten all kinds of things.

How to eat cake and how to run and how to tell stories.

What's going on? Why is everything so hard all of a sudden?

Grandma was sitting up straight in a white bed on wheels with
a kind of fence around it.

Maia thought she was sitting much too still.

Grandma stared at the TV
all day long. Maia couldn't
take it any more. She
stamped her foot. And when
that didn't help, she kicked
one of the wheels of the bed.
So what if it hurts? I don't care!
The bed wobbled for a
moment. But nothing
changed. So Maia started
drawing pictures to put on
the bare walls. She made
wonky things to put on the
bedside cabinet and a
plate for cake.

Maia did a thousand drawings for the walls, and she made
a thousand wonky things to put on the bedside cabinet.
She filled the room to overflowing, and the nurses got angry.
They grumbled that it was a hospital, for goodness' sake,
not a playroom.
And they said they couldn't find a thing in there.
Maia just shrugged.

Blah-blah. They can't tell me what to do. I'll draw a ship.

'Fip,' said Grandma.

Maia drew a bird.

'Sird,' said Grandma, and her mouth dragged on the right.

Maia's mother didn't understand what Grandma was saying,
and Grandpa just pretended.
They answered 'yes' when it should have been 'no', and 'no'
when it should have been 'yes'.
They gave her soup when she wanted potatoes.

Isn't anyone listening?

She asked for chips and steak! Have you got cake in your ears?

Maia knew exactly what Grandma was saying. She read it in her
eyes and picked the letters out of Grandma's mouth. Very carefully.
Because Grandma had grown slow. Very, very slow.
And then something else happened.

Grandpa died.

Maia was there when her mother found him, so no one needed to lie.

Grandpa was sitting in his easy chair.

He's sitting so still.

He hadn't broken anything except the cup of tea he was drinking.

The pieces lay at his feet.

On the carpet. On that beautiful carpet!

His eyes were shut and he was smiling, as if someone had just said
something funny.

Grandpa had broken a teacup and stopped living.

Lots of things needed arranging. Mum phoned, wrote, ran,
and blew her nose in thousands of tissues.
Maia went to see Grandma. First Grandma's eyes got wet,
then her cheeks, then her dress. Maia didn't have enough hands
to hold back all those tears.

Soon the whole room will be flooded!

The floor got wet. Next thing, the bed would float out the door.

Then we'll sail all the way to China.

When everything had dried again, Grandma said she wanted to see Grandpa.
To run her fingers through his hair one last time. That was all.
The nurse shook her head. She said it wasn't possible.
Maia got angry.

Out of the way, you silly goose. If you won't help, we'll do it ourselves!

'Right,' said Grandma.

Right!

And Grandma climbed over the fence.

It was cold where Grandpa was. So cold that white clouds came out of Maia's mouth and out of Grandma's too.

How pretty. How incredibly beautiful.

Maia pushed Grandma's chair up next to the coffin. There weren't any clouds coming out of Grandpa's mouth. His eyes were shut and he was still smiling.

'Bye,' said Grandma, stroking his wiry hair. Then she smiled at Maia.

'Cake,' she said.

Petits Fours

2C, Rue Saint-Sulpice

PARIS

, Rue Saint-Sulpice

PA

PARIS

28, Rue

plce

28

Petits Fours